Tennis

A Level Two Reader

By Cynthia Klingel and Robert B. Noyed

The Child's World®

Back and forth. Back and forth. You must be watching a tennis match!

Anyone can play tennis. You need a tennis racket and a tennis ball. You can practice by hitting against a wall.

Tennis games are called matches. They are played on a tennis court.

A racket is used to hit the ball. The strings in the racket are tight.

You play tennis with a small, fuzzy ball. A tennis ball bounces very easily.

Players hit the ball back and forth across the net. They try to hit the ball so the other player cannot hit it back.

13

Tennis can be played with two players. One player is on each side of the net. This is called a singles match.

Tennis can also be played with four players. Two players are on each side of the net. This is called a doubles match.

Tennis takes good hitting skills and attention. Tennis players need to think quickly.

Being a good tennis player takes practice. But you can have fun even if you are a beginner!

Index

To Find Out More

Books

Bailey, Donna. *Tennis.* Austin, Tex.: Raintree/Steck-Vaughn, 1991.

Crossingham, John, and Bonna Rouse. *Tennis in Action.* New York: Crabtree Publications Company, 2002.

Dexter, Robin, and R. W. Alley. *Young Arthur Ashe: Brave Champion.* Mahwah, N.J.: Troll Association, 1996.

Sherman, Josepha. *Venus Williams.* Chicago: Heinemann Library, 2001.

Web Sites

Visit our homepage for lots of links about tennis:
http://www.childsworld.com/links.html

Note to Parents, Teachers, and Librarians:
We routinely verify our Web links to make sure they're safe, active sites—so encourage your readers to check them out!

Note to Parents and Educators

Welcome to Wonder Books®! These books provide text at three different levels for beginning readers to practice and strengthen their reading skills. Additionally, the use of nonfiction text provides readers the valuable opportunity to *read to learn*, not just to learn to read.

These leveled readers allow children to choose books at their level of reading confidence and performance. Nonfiction Level One books offer beginning readers simple language, word choice, and sentence structure as well as a word list. Nonfiction Level Two books feature slightly more difficult vocabulary, longer sentences, and longer total text. In the back of each Nonfiction Level Two book are an index and a list of books and Web sites for finding out more information. Nonfiction Level Three books continue to extend word choice and length of text. In the back of each Nonfiction Level Three book are a glossary, an index, and a list of books and Web sites for further research.

State and national standards in reading and language arts emphasize using nonfiction at all levels of reading development. Wonder Books® fill the historical void in nonfiction material for primary grade readers with the additional benefit of a leveled text.

About the Authors

Cynthia Klingel has worked as a high school English teacher and an elementary school teacher. She is currently the curriculum director for a Minnesota school district. Cynthia lives with her family in Mankato, Minnesota.

Robert B. Noyed started his career as a newspaper reporter. Since then, he has worked in school communications and public relations at the state and national level. Robert lives with his family in Brooklyn Center, Minnesota.

Readers should remember…
All sports carry a certain amount of risk. To reduce the risk of injury while playing tennis, play at your own level, wear all safety gear, and use care and common sense. The publisher and author take no responsibility or liability for injuries resulting from playing tennis.

Published by The Child's World®
P.O. Box 326
Chanhassen, MN 55317-0326
800-599-READ
www.childsworld.com

Photo Credits
© AFP/CORBIS: 2
© Bob Thomas/GettyImages: 6
© Dennis MacDonald/PhotoEdit: 13
© Eyewire/GettyImages: cover
© George Shelley/CORBIS: 5, 10
© Royalty-Free/CORBIS: 9, 18
© Royalty-Free/GettyImages: 17
© R. W. Jones/CORBIS: 14
© Ziggy Kaluzny/Tony Stone: 21

Editorial Directions, Inc.: E. Russell Primm and Emily J. Dolbear, Editors;
Alice K. Flanagan, Photo Researcher

The Child's World®: Mary Berendes, Publishing Director

Library of Congress Cataloging-in-Publication Data
Klingel, Cynthia Fitterer.
Tennis / by Cynthia Klingel and Robert B. Noyed.
p. cm. — (Wonder books, an easy reader)
Summary: Simple text describes the sport of tennis, how it is played, and the equipment used.
Includes bibliographical references and index.
ISBN 1-56766-462-8 (lib bdg. : alk. paper)
1. Tennis—Juvenile literature. [1. Tennis.] I. Noyed, Robert B. II. Title. III. Wonder books (Chanhassen, Minn.)
GV996.5.K55 2003
796.342—dc21   2002015150